Light Skinned
Thoughts

Experiences In Colorism

Tamekia Jackson

Illustrated by Graphexx

Light Skinned Thoughts
Tamekia Jackson

ISBN: 978-1-7371738-2-3
Published by Tamekia Jackson

Dedication

For every black and brown child that struggles with their skin tone for various reasons.

This book was written to bring awareness to individuals about how colorism affects our youth.

Knowing and correcting it with our children in the early stages, can brighten their future everyday lives.

They are our future.

Parents and Guardians

This book is a guide to show you what your children may be thinking when it comes to colorism.

It can help children of all ages and allow them to be more conscious of the way they look at others.

Acknowledgments

I would like to give special thanks to my Father, God Almighty, for giving me the vision and courage to write this book to bring awareness to colorism among our youth.

I would also like to thank my husband, Emanuel, for supporting and believing in my many endeavors. A great big hug and kiss to my loving son Elijah for sharing his mommy with the writing of this book.

Thanks to my parents for giving me life. And last but not least, thanks to my beautiful sister Serenthia for always guiding me and bringing out the beauty in me. I still love her skin tone today, but I now view my darker complexion as regal and one of a kind.

Light Skinned
Thoughts

Experiences In Colorism

Grow some hair, baldie!

You look like a monkey!

You look mean!

Why are your gums black?

Why is your hair so nappy?

On the previous page, whom do you think these remarks are referring to? Explain your answer.

....

....

....

When you look in the mirror, are you happy or sad?
Explain your answer.

....

....

....

Why can't I have lighter skin?

Why do I feel dirty?

Why am I not pretty?

Why do I have dark skin and a big nose?

#Why #Why #Why

Do you ever have these or similar thoughts? If so, explain.

....

....

....

....

I wish I could wear different colored contact lenses.

I wish I could wear different colored lipsticks and not look like a clown

I wish I was beautiful like my sister.

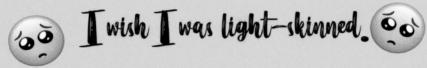

I wish I was light-skinned.

#I wish #I wish #I wish

Do you wish you looked different? If so, explain.

....

....

....

....

If you could change one thing about yourself,
what would it be and why?

....

....

....

My daughter is cute to be dark-skinned.
Dark-skinned people are mean.
Sugar
flour;
ALL PURPOSE

Do you feel like dark-skinned people are mean or ugly?
Whether yes or no, please explain.

....

....

....

Has a family member or anyone you looked up to ever called you a name that made you feel uncomfortable in your skin? Please explain your answer.

....

....

....

WHY CAN'T I GET THIS DIRT OFF OF ME!!

I'm going to become clean once and for all !

Maybe, I'll get more likes on social media.

Maybe, I can eventually wear different colored lipstick and wigs.

Maybe, my dad will think I'm pretty like my sister.

#Maybe #Maybe #JustMaybe

Have you ever tried to change your complexion?
If so, how and why?

....

....

....

All SHADES Matter

6ft

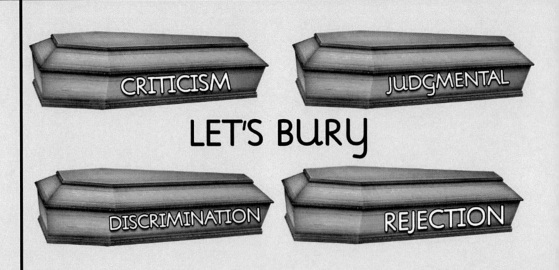

CRITICISM

JUDGMENTAL

LET'S BURY

DISCRIMINATION

REJECTION

I serve a God of fresh starts and new beginnings (2 Cor. 5:17).

Just know, whatever shade you are, we are all masterpieces created by God (Eph. 2:20).

Look at yourself in the mirror and tell yourself, "I will be the first person of color to?"

....

....

....

....

Daily Positive Affirmations. Repeat your affirmation seven times.

....

....

....

....

....

....

....

....

....

....

....

....

....

....

....

....

Colorism

Colorism is a form of internalized racism that we feel toward ourselves and others.

It's a prejudice or discrimination, especially within a racial or ethnic group, favoring people with lighter skin over those with darker skin.

Do you like your complexion? Why or why not?

....

....

....

Do you see your complexion as better, worse, or the same as others? Explain your answer.

....

....

....

....

How would you feel if you heard a person of color teasing someone else of the same color about their complexion?

....

....

....

What can you do to help colorism go away?

....

....

....

Write a list of what's beautiful about you. Example: your hair, your skin complexion, your personality, etc.

....

....

....

Parents/Guardians

Now you have an idea of your child's thoughts and feelings concerning colorism. How can you help them overcome their issues? Let's help change the mindset of one child at a time. Colorism is real. Let's create a solution and be a part of an evolution!

Let's: Eliminate colorism among ourselves.

Create different platforms on social media groups, community functions, and anything else that will help our youth come together to know that all shades are equal and beautiful.

Never make people of one complexion feel beneath those of another. Let's be conscious of our thought processes when it comes to our stereotypical ways of thinking. Love ourselves and others the way we were created. Find beauty in our unique Nubian skin.

Note: Parents/Guardians, please be mindful of how we speak and act in front of our children.

ALL SHADES MATTER!

I Am

I am regal!

My dark skin makes me royalty!

I am spontaneous!

I live without fear!

I can do all things!

I embrace my culture!

I am beautiful!

I am a child of God!

I love myself!

I absolutely LOVE the skin I'm in!

Your Turn

I am...

....

....

I can..

....

....

I absolutely LOVE (about myself)

....

....

Assignment

In the next 48 hours, give at least three people of color a compliment.

Once Completed: How did it feel being part of a positive solution to colorism?

....

....

....

....

Made in the USA
Monee, IL
30 December 2021

86053747R00021